I0534114

Postmodern Fragments
Writings on Work, Technology and Contemporary Living

Christopher Nosnibor

Clinicality Press
York
England

Postmodern Fragments:
Writings on Work, Technology and Contemporary Living

Copyright © 2008 Christopher Nosnibor

Published 2008 by Clinicality Press, York.
http://clinicalitypress.co.uk

All rights reserved.

http://christophernosnibor.co.uk

http://www.myspace.com/christophernosnibor

ISBN 978-0-9556939-1-5

At Home He's a Tourist: Reconsidering the Postmodern Condition

So after completing both a very long project (I'm talking the best part of a decade) and 'The Worker' within a week of one another, it was time for a few days off. This isn't one of my greatest skills, so Mrs Nosnibor and I took off for a short break in Whitby. Knowing that I find it very difficult to stop – if there's a keyboard to be tapped, you can bet all the money you've ever seen that I'll be itching to type, to get some ideas down, or to flesh out an idea I've had previously but not had the opportunity to work through. Well, I am a writing machine... and it's for this reason that when asked if we should take the laptop (strictly speaking it's Mrs Nosnibor's laptop, given that I have a PC and a whole room in which to use it, but still) I said no. I wanted a proper break. I had no idea how difficult it would be. (That said, the fact I did pack a notepad – the likes of which I take everywhere I go – and a pen suggests that perhaps subconsciously I had an inkling.)

I'm pleased to report that I didn't commit a single word to paper (postcards excepted). But then, the postcards I sent to my immediate family got me back to thinking about something I've been musing a fair bit lately, namely the ways in which we communicate, and how technology has impacted upon them. And, more broadly, about how current technologies have changed the way we conduct relationships, and, indeed, our daily lives. Normally, if I'm not typing furiously, I'm constantly checking my emails, my blog hits, my eBay listings, my website... the list goes on.

Such fidgeting can only be a contemporary phenomenon. Of course, I daresay people have been restless and bursting with energy that gets channelled into pointless activity for millennia, but the constant refreshing of pages has to have originated with the Internet. Ok, so this isn't necessarily 'postmodern' per se – Lyotard's seminal text *The Postmodern Condition* is concerned with the organisation and status of knowledge. But he also linked the changing status of 'narrative' and the legitimation of 'knowledge' to late capitalism and the rapid flow of information that corresponds with this postindustrial age. And the way information is transmitted is now very different when compared with the time when Lyotard was writing in the late 1970s, and, indeed, with any other time in history. People text. People email. People send photographs by email. They send them by text. Are the days of postcards numbered? I certainly hope not, and my sending of postcards was as much a ritual gesture as a means of relaying important information concerning my whereabouts.

But why should I – or anyone else, other than, perhaps, anyone in the industries connected to postcards – be concerned? Is not mourning the demise of the postcard simply a pointless and, indeed, spurious nostalgia trip, another aspect of a yearning for a golden age that never really was? Aye, it were grand, back int' day when life were sepiatoned and looked just like t' Hovis ads, son. Actually, no. I'm dealing with deeper, and broader issues here, namely concerning the ways in which we communicate overall.

Consider the following questions: How much time do you get for leisure? You time? For socialising? Ok, so you probably have responsibilities - job, family, general living, by which I mean cooking, eating, washing, etc., etc. – and how much time away from these do you get? Yes, *leisure* time. That's time to do as you please, things you enjoy doing. Time spent participating in activities that aren't a chore.

Technology was supposed to give us more leisure time, but it seems to be having the opposite result. There can be no question that there are more labour-saving devices in existence now than ever before. Things like washing, washing up even eating, take next to no time in comparison to in times past. You've never had it so good! And distance is no object. With the advent of the Internet, it's as easy to keep in touch with someone on the other side of the globe as it is someone who lives on the next street. You don't have to leave the house for either, and in both cases it's instant. In short, communication has never been easier. Or faster. It's instant. But this immediacy has exacerbated the demand everything, and demand it yesterday, culture of impatience. And there's the rub. Communication is too easy. Talk is cheap. Quality is falling by the wayside: quantity rules. And there's no escape. People arrive at work and are overwhelmed by the sheer volume of emails waiting them. A recent survey found that people working from home work the equivalent of an extra 20 days a year, which almost counters their holiday entitlement. The technology that has facilitated what would first appear to be the perfect working solution and the best way to obtain a more comfortable work/life balance is thus a double-edged sword. Small wonder people don't all want to rush home and check their inbox.

I see it all the time on MySpace: people send out bulletins or update their status to apologise for not keeping up with blogs or responding to comments and messages because they're so 'busy.' I've experienced it myself: you subscribe to so many blogs, it's impossible to read and comment on them all, despite the best intentions. And the same goes for email: news letters, order updates, not to mention the reams and reams of spam... Be honest: how many times have you been gripped by fear at the prospect of logging in and checking your email, because of the idea of dealing with hassling correspondence from the bank and a slew of messages from people you can't face replying to is simply too much? Email and mobile communications technology was hailed as a great means of keeping people in touch with one another. But how many proper emails do you send or receive?

As someone who has, at various points in my life been a big letter writer, I probably send too few 'proper' emails myself these days, but receive even fewer. And of those I receive, it's rare for them to extend beyond three lines now. Abundant forwards and links, but no personal input. No conversation. Seemingly, conversation is dead.

So what are the implications? For starters, it would seem that friendships function on a different level and in a different way from before. Just as postmodern literature is often said to be typified by discontinuous narrative forms and rapid narrative switches, reflecting the kind of rapid-cut MTV videos that assume that the average attention span is in the region of 8 seconds, so people communicate in soundbites, abbreviated exchanges made in an abbreviated language, in terms of both vocabulary and spelling. Which suggests that perhaps the average attention span is in the region of 8 seconds. But is this a cause or effect? It's hard to say: it's hard to determine, and even harder to differentiate.

So, when I'm not immersed in the creation of dazzling texts that combine fiction with editorial and striving to encapsulate the agonies of contemporary living in genre-defying narratives, eating cheese, growing chillies or brewing beer, I try to maintain contact with my friends. But it's increasingly difficult. And that's why I'm on both sides of the fence where the technology's concerned. My criticisms are made as a very vocal fan of the social and interactive potentials of the Internet. I try – harder than most – to maintain contact with people. But it has to be reciprocal, and I've lost many friends – good friends – because of the one-sidedness that often develops in a relationship. I'm patient, but I have my limits. Perhaps it's in part on account of my age, and the age of my friends, my peers. Even the ones who aren't devoting their time to creating the next generation are all incredibly busy. Careers, house purchasing and renovating... so no, they don't want to go to the pub or a gig, and they don't have time to type more than a couple of lines. And I feel like a kid who's disgruntled because no-one wants to come out to play. Perhaps I'm confusing the ageing process from the perspective of a social misfit with the effects of technology on communication. Well, no, not really. It's the same society that's driven my peers to believe that a career, owning a home and all the rest is the course that life takes.

There's a fair amount of research that now suggests that midlife crises occur earlier now than in previous generations. Explanations vary, but there's a general consensus that the pressure of the expectation of success at an earlier age (as precipitated by .com boomers and the like) is the primary contributing factor. Whether the circumstance has come from people and been amplified by the media, or has been perpetuated by the media and thus become an actuality is irrelevant: the end result is the same. No-one seems to have any time. They're consumed by the need to get somewhere, literally and metaphorically. But no-one seems to be enjoying the journey. Which, to me, seems to be missing the point. You may never get where you want to, so might as well make the most of the route there.

Interaction is – was – a significant feature of that journey. The people you meet along the way don't only have the capacity to provide interesting diversions and entertainment, but can also be invaluable sources of knowledge. By closing off the channels of deeper discourse with others, people are turning down the opportunity to develop, on so many levels. On the one hand, our 'fragmented' postmodern culture makes it increasingly difficult to make interpersonal connections. 'Clicking' with people is hard, and the less like everyone else you are, the harder and rarer it is. The more diverse your interests, the fewer will share them all. Which leaves the options of increased isolation, or a taking a wider selection of half-friends who share some of those interests in great detail. But on the other hand, because of networking sites like MySpace, it's easier than ever before to locate people who share less mainstream interests and literary or musical tastes. But again, that requires an investment of time – time that many feel they do not have.

Of course, there's no substitute for face to face, down the pub meanderings. But strangely, I feel that right now I have more detailed discussion taking place on my blogs, with people I've never met, than many of the people I've known in 'real life' for years, the ones who don't have time to email because they have a career or whatever (although overseas holidays can usually be accommodated. One of the perks of a career is income... but then, it's equally conceivable that the holiday is as much 'expected' as the car and three-bed house). I'm not sure if that's entirely a good thing, or entirely a bad thing. It's certainly better than no discussion.

This discussion – or, as is perhaps more common for people now, absence of discussion – has a direct impact on the issue of knowledge, the focus of *The Postmodern Condition*. Discussion fuels a discourse of engagement, which leads to the formation of individual opinion (assuming the individual possesses at least some degree of capacity for thought). The Internet is, unquestionably, the greatest – by which I mean the largest and most readily accessible – resource for information in existence, and probably in history. But obtaining information solely from the Internet doesn't demand discussion or the exchange of contrasting perspectives. It's isn't interactive – not really. And like any resource for information, it requires research to obtain detailed information from a broad range of sources, and a lot of effort – and critical consideration – to extrapolate the real facts and to draw a balanced, objective version of things. There's a lot of opinion out there. There's a lot of half-arsed, poorly researched and downright ill-informed opinion out there. There's also a lot of misinformation and propaganda. Of course, it was ever thus: the mass media (and the underground media, too) was always about the shaping of opinions through the manipulation of language and information, about the (mis)use of narrative for specific ends. Now, however, there is more. Much more. And no-one really has time to verify the accuracy or legitimacy of the 'knowledge' being transmitted: certain agencies – such as the BBC, for example – are invested with a degree of authority that's rarely questioned. Wikipedia is a prime example of an agency which has attained a status of legitimacy which is often questionable, even spurious at times, but which is rarely actually questioned. Factual inaccuracies can thus traverse the globe at improbable speed and become gospel unchallenged. Which is quite dangerous: even the most reliable sources are fallible.

Equally concerningly, we can see that in the current climate, because no-one has any time, it's common to refer to only a small, select number of sources for information, be it news, film or music reviews, even downloads or on-line shopping. So, while the fragmentation of culture and society that leading critics (I'm thinking in terms of literature here, so mean Eagleton, Hutcheon, Jameson) identify as being a defining feature of postmodernity has undeniably occurred, a surfeit of choice has had the inverse effect, namely the homogenisation of culture. It's for this reason that independent shops are going to the wall on a daily basis, while Tesco and Wal-Mart march on toward global domination. As do Google, Microsoft, Intel, etc., etc.. People go for what they've heard of, and like to get everything in the one place. Because they're lazy? Or because they haven't got time? A bit of both, probably. Precisely how things will evolve in the future is near impossible to predict, but already it feels like a different world from that Lyotard observed, and I can't help but feel that we're entering the post-postmodern age.

The Worker

1. Every Day is Like Sunday.

Sunday morning. Hangover. Took him a moment to realise where he was. Home. His own bed. A good sign. Fully dressed. He glanced around, the movement of his eyeballs in their sockets making him wince in pain. The pungent aroma of the previous night's smoke which clung to his clothes, mingled with the sickly-sweet tartness of stale sweat made his stomach lurch, but he observed with relieve that his bed was free of puke and he's not pissed or shat himself either. Ok, so it was rare for either of those things to happen, but they weren't unheard of. How had he got home? And when? Where had he been, even? After arriving at the club, already hammered, some time after ten or thereabouts, everything was a blank. He felt like shit, felt like he was gonna die.

He moaned and gingerly winched himself out of bed. Went to the bathroom, pissed like a horse for a good couple of minutes. Bliss! Chugged half a pint of full-fat milk straight from the carton, threw down some painkillers and tossed some bread in the toaster. Checked the clock. Ok, so it wasn't Sunday morning any more, it was closer to 1pm. A seriously heavy night. He buttered the hot toast on ejection from the machine and took a couple of bites before a wave of nausea broke from the pit of his stomach. He made haste back to the bathroom and spewed it all back up. mouth, nose, some serious velocity. He wiped his mouth with the back of his hand and crawled back to bed.

The next time he woke it was just after 3pm. He still felt rough, but nothing like the way he had felt before. What a waste of a day. Still in the clothes from the night before, he went back to the kitchen and prepared a mammoth fried breakfast and sat in front of the television while he troughed down the greasy collation. There was a match on. He didn't really give a shit about Liverpool or Chelsea, being a Man U supporter but football's football.

Afternoon rolled into evening as he sat, vegetating, on the sofa. Fuck it, he couldn't be arsed to wash up or so any washing, not today. It would keep. Around 8, he decided to take a shower, after which, still wrapped in his towel, he fired up the PC and checked his emails. Nothing much doing. He logged into his Facebook account. A few tagged pics from last night were up already, and a number of people had left him comments, too. But as far as he could ascertain, he'd only danced like a twat and tried cracking onto a couple of birds, both absolute munters, by all accounts. But he'd not screwed either of them – because they'd turned him down flat – and he'd not flashed his cock or arse, so on balance, no cause for concern. He idly flipped up some porn pages. Before long, his horn was throbbing as hard as his head had been earlier in the day, and he knocked out a mix over a couple of chicks lezzing it up. Job done, he wiped himself down, put the telly on and watched some second-rate eighties action movie till just gone midnight. Waste of a day, alright, but it sure as hell beat having to go to work.

2. I Don't Like Mondays

The harsh buzz of the alarm sliced through the darkness and penetrated his dark place, his sleeping brain. He woke and was momentarily groggy before the realisation hits: Monday morning. 7:30. He hit the snooze button and buried his head in the pillow once more. Under the duvet, it was warm and comfortable and life was good. But the alarm persisted and he forced himself to vacate his haven.

He dressed, ate breakfast, brushed his hair, cleaned his teeth. He was running late, so no time for a shave today. 8:25 and he's having to run to make the 8:30 bus: the bus-stop is an eight and a half minute walk but he can make it in half that at a run. He hates running, because he's not fit – too much beer, too many cigarettes – and he hates arriving at work an exhausted ball of sweat. But he can't be late, he's been late too many times recently and his timekeeping has become an issue. He's already on a first warning.

8:59 and he's in the office, firing up his workstation, positioning his chair, the usual routine. The phone rang. He took the call, went through the scripted schpiel, dispensed some pointless information to the frustrated old goat at the other end of the line, updated the systems, shunted some papers around. Rinse and repeat. The phone rang. He took the call. Etc. Such is the daily grind of the 9-5. Why did he put up with it? Because there was nothing else. He needed to eat, to keep a roof over his head, pay the bills. It's the white man's burden alright.

Necessity is the mother of surrendering one's dreams to grim reality. He was looking for a job and then he found a job, with prospects and benefits, so his interviewer, smug in his navy pinstripe suit and tan shoes had informed him. But it soon became apparent that the corporate ladder was all a con, and worse, a trap. A stop-gap job becomes a career.

The calls kept on coming and the papers kept on piling up, and while he was on the rota for taking his lunch hour from 12:30 to 13:30, he was stuck on a call with some irate customer and wasn't able to get away until 12:50. But then, the phones were supposed to be manned by a certain number of staff - 10, equating to 50% of the team - at any given time, and the workshy heifer at the next desk was late back from her lunch.

He was getting hungry and struggled to contain his frustration. It was the same pretty much every day and the days had a tendency to run together, like watercolours on saturated paper. Another cup of rancid instant coffee as stagnant as his life, another plastic spoon, another whinging tosser, the hours passed into days passed into weeks passed into months passed into years, a wasted life, an accidental career. All the other jobs advertised locally were much of a muchness. No, the only way out was redundancy or retirement. Or death. He found it hard to rouse any sense of optimism. Too long in the rut, his spirit had been ground down and eventually crushed, all sense of hope extinguished. They owned him and he knew it.

Lunch: he nipped out to the sandwich shop at the top of the street, bought a nutritionally vapid chicken salad sandwich on flaccid white bread. The chicken was dry, anaemic, the salad wilted to fuck. Sluiced it down with a can of Coke. He could ill afford to dine this way as he was well in the red and pay-day was still a fortnight off, but he simply couldn't find the motivation to prepare a packed lunch.

His truncated lunch hour – he had to be back by 13:00, and while some of his colleagues were capable of getting away with pulling epic skives and late sign-ins, he was neither comfortable with nor in a position to do the same – was over all too soon and he returned to his desk, signed back into his terminal and the onslaught, the grind continued. The influx of work – phone calls, emails, paper correspondence – demanding his attention was ceaseless. 5:30 seemed a long way off.

An hour later and his bladder was growing taught. He desperately needed to piss, but there was simply no respite. He was also tired, so tired. More cups of gut-rotting instant coffee was the only means available of fending off this terminal fatigue.

5:30 rolled around eventually, he switched off his workstation, clocked off, took a long, long piss that felt like heaven, and left the building. He didn't have log to wait for a bus home. On arrival, he cracked open a can of beer. It didn't last long. What to eat? There wasn't much in. His funds were low and he'd not had the cash or motivation to make the trip to the supermarket at the weekend. A sad, salt-heavy microwave meal for one sat brooding in the back of the cupboard, so he nuked the plastic tray and chowed down the stodgy collation without enthusiasm, washed it down with a second can of lager. It was piss, but it was cold and alcoholic.

He flicked on the TV and vegetated in front of a series of mundane lifestyle and 'talent' shows with a couple more tins. Midnight rolled around and he decided it was time to hit the sack. He needed to sleep: there was work tomorrow.

3. Ruby Tuesday, or, Tuesday's gonna be the day that they're gonna throw it back to you

Shit! How long has the alarm been going? He must've been sound asleep. The harsh buzz of the alarm slices through the darkness and sears his sleeping brain. He sits upright with a start and checks the clock: 7:52. He hit the snooze button and buried his head in the pillow, but it was no good. Under the duvet, it was warm and comfortable and life was good. But the alarm persisted and he forced himself to vacate his haven. He dressed, ate breakfast, brushed his hair, cleaned his teeth. He was running late, so no time for a shave today. 8:25 and he's having to run to make the 8:30 bus: the bus-stop is an eight and a half minute walk but he can make it in half that at a run. He hates running, because he's not fit - too much beer, too many cigarettes - and he hates arriving at work an exhausted ball of sweat. But he can't be late, he's been late too many times recently and his timekeeping has become an issue. He's already on a first warning.

8:59 and he's in the office, firing up his workstation, positioning his chair, the usual routine. The phone rang. He took the call, went through the scripted schpiel, dispensed some pointless information to the frustrated old goat at the other end of the line, updated the systems, shunted some papers around. Rinse and repeat. The phone rang. He took the call. Etc. Such is the daily grind of the 9-5.

The calls kept on coming and the papers kept on piling up, and while he was on the rota for taking his lunch hour from 12:30 to 13:30, he was stuck on a call with some irate customer and wasn't able to get away until 12:50. But then, the phones were supposed to be manned by a certain number of staff - 10, equating to 50% of the team - at any given time, and the workshy heifer at the next desk was late back from her lunch. His boss was circling like a shark. He couldn't fathom why the power-hungry corporate tosser had taken such a dislike to him, but it seemed as though he was on a mission. He has to watch his back: one step out of line and the boss would be on him, and could bring him down. He'd seen it done before.

He was getting hungry and struggled to contain his frustration. It was the same pretty much every day and the days had a tendency to run together, like watercolours on saturated paper. Another cup of rancid instant coffee as stagnant as his life, another plastic spoon, another whinging tosser, the hours passed into days passed into weeks passed into months passed into years, a wasted life, an accidental career. All the other jobs advertised locally were much of a muchness. No, the only way out was redundancy or retirement. Or death. He found it hard to rouse any sense of optimism. Too long in the rut, his spirit had been ground down and eventually crushed, all sense of hope extinguished. They owned him and he knew it.

Lunch: he nipped out to the sandwich shop at the top of the street, bought a nutritionally vapid ham salad sandwich on flaccid white bread. The ham was dry, anaemic, the salad wilted to fuck. Sluiced it down with a can of Tango. He could ill afford to dine this way as he was well in the red and pay-day was still a fortnight off, but he simply couldn't find the motivation to prepare a packed lunch.

His truncated lunch hour – he had to be back by 13:00, and while some of his colleagues were capable of getting away with pulling epic skives and late sign-ins, he was neither comfortable with nor in a position to do the same – was over all too soon and he returned to his desk, signed back into his terminal and the onslaught, the grind continued. The influx of work – phone calls, emails, paper correspondence – demanding his attention was ceaseless. 5:30 seemed a long way off.

An hour later and his bladder was growing taught. He desperately needed to piss, but there was simply no respite. He was also tired, so tired. More cups of gut-rotting instant coffee was the only means available of fending off this terminal fatigue.

5:30 rolled around eventually, he switched off his workstation, clocked off, took a long, long piss that felt like heaven, and left the building. He didn't have log to wait for a bus home. On arrival, he cracked open a can of beer. It didn't last long. What to eat? There wasn't much in. His funds were low and he'd not had the cash or motivation to make the trip to the supermarket at the weekend. A sad, salt-heavy microwave meal for one sat brooding in the back of the cupboard, so he nuked the plastic tray and chowed down the stodgy collation without enthusiasm, washed it down with a second can of lager. It was piss, but it was cold and alcoholic.

He flicked on the TV but there was fuck all on so he fired up the PC and surfed for porn. A quick one off the wrist and then idled away the remainder of the evening on Facebook and a couple more tins. Midnight rolled around and he decided it was time to hit the sack. He needed to sleep: there was work tomorrow.

4. Wednesday Morning 3am

Holy fuck! He awoke with a start. He had been deep in sleep, in the middle of some long and winding epic dream. There had been some crazy alarms and sirens, fires everywhere and bombs dropping.... but in a jolting instant he realised that the alarm of his dream had been the alarm clock by the bed. How long ha it been going? He checks the time: 8:02. Fuck, shit, bollocks, bugger fuck cunt, he's going to have to get a move on. He hauled his arse out of bed and threw on yesterday's clothes that were strewn at the foot of the bed. No time for breakfast – he'd used up the last of the milk yesterday and hadn't made it to the supermarket since – he brushed his hair, cleaned his teeth. He was running late, so no time for a shave today. 8:27 and he's having to run to make the 8:30 bus: the bus-stop is an eight and a half minute walk but he can make it in half that at a run. He hates running, because he's not fit - too much beer, too many cigarettes - and he hates arriving at work an exhausted ball of sweat. But he can't be late. He's in luck: the bus is running a couple of minutes late, and he arrives, panting and thoroughly fagged out just as it pulls up.

9:00 on the dot and he's made it to the office, firing up his workstation, positioning his chair, the usual routine. The phone rang. He took the call, went through the scripted schpiel, dispensed some pointless information to the frustrated old goat at the other end of the line, updated the systems, shunted some papers around. Rinse and repeat. The phone rang. He took the call. Etc. Such is the daily grind of the 9-5.

The calls kept on coming and the papers kept on piling up, and while he was on the rota for taking his lunch hour from 12:30 to 13:30, he was stuck on a call with some irate customer and wasn't able to get away until 12:50. But then, the phones were supposed to be manned by a certain number of staff – 10, equating to 50% of the team – at any given time, and the workshy heifer at the next desk was late back from her lunch. When she did arrive, he noted with disdain just how badly she was starting to smell, a side-effect of her fucked-up interpretation of the Atkins diet. As she ploughed her way through a large bag of pork scratchings, he paused when she realised he was clocking her, his face conveying a disgust and disbelief it was hard to disguise. She explained – not for the first time, and with a cloud of deep-fried and seasoned pork rind gusting from her chops as she spoke – that she could eat all the fats she wanted, but absolutely no carbs. Sure. His boss was circling like a shark. He couldn't fathom why the power-hungry corporate tosser had taken such a dislike to him, but it seemed as though he was on a mission. He has to watch his back: one step out of line and the boss would be on him, and could bring him down. He'd seen it done before.

He was getting hungry and struggled to contain his frustration. It was the same pretty much every day and the days had a tendency to run together, like watercolours on saturated paper. He could feel himself getting down. He was in a rut and he knew it. Same shit, different day and no mistake: every day drains into the next, and every day is exactly the same. Could be worse, he reminded himself. It was only work, after all, not his life. His evenings and weekends were his own, at least. Please give me evenings and weekends...

Lunch: he nipped out to the sandwich shop at the top of the street, bought a nutritionally vapid ham salad sandwich on flaccid white bread. The ham was dry, anaemic, the salad wilted to fuck. Sluiced it down with a can of Tango. He could ill afford to dine this way as he was well in the red and pay-day was still a fortnight off, but he simply couldn't find the motivation to prepare a packed lunch.

His truncated lunch hour – he had to be back by 13:30, and while some of his colleagues were capable of getting away with pulling epic skives and late sign-ins, he was neither comfortable with nor in a position to do the same – was over all too soon and he returned to his desk, signed back into his terminal and the onslaught, the grind continued. The influx of work – phone calls, emails, paper correspondence – demanding his attention was ceaseless. 5:30 seemed a long way off.

The cleaner came round on her weekly circuit, with a bucket containing a couple of inches of fetid brown water and a Jaycloth, which she proceeded to smear over each desk in turn, before lifting the receiver of any phone not in use - or even phones in use if headsets were plugged in - and wiping the mouth and earpieces with the same crutty cloth. No rinse, only repeat: six, eight, ten desks and telephones would get this once-over before the encrusted cloth was returned to the bucket for a brief swill.

5:30 rolled around eventually, he switched off his workstation, clocked off, took a long, long piss that felt like heaven, and left the building. He'd hoped to get a couple of pints in after work, but Steve was taking his girlfriend out for a meal and Simon had his mum coming round. At the bus stop, his bowels started growling. He didn't have log to wait for a bus home, but it got stuck in traffic. Discomfort began to nudge at his lower abdomen. The jam seemed to last forever, and he was practically touching cloth by the time he got home. He threw his jacket over the back of the sofa and went to curl one out. The relief!

Movements complete, he cracked open a can of beer. It didn't last long. What to eat? There wasn't much in. His funds were low and he'd not had the cash or motivation to make the trip to the supermarket at the weekend. A sad, salt-heavy microwave meal for one sat brooding in the back of the cupboard, so he nuked the plastic tray and chowed down the stodgy collation without enthusiasm, washed it down with a second can of lager. It was piss, but it was cold and alcoholic. He wanted more, so nipped round to the offy a couple of streets away and stuck a couple of four-packs on special on his credit card. He'd worry about paying it off later.

Cracking open the first of the eight fresh cans, he flicked on the TV but there was fuck all on so he fired up the PC and surfed for porn. He whipped up a serving of cream, then idled away the remainder of the evening on Facebook and another half dozen tins. Midnight rolled around and rather worse for wear, he decided it was time to hit the sack. He needed to sleep: there was work tomorrow.

5. Thursday Afternoon (edit)

The harsh buzz of the alarm slices through the darkness and sears his sleeping brain. He sits up and checks the clock: 7:30. He hits the snooze button, but is surprisingly awake for this time of day. Perhaps as well. He has to be up and out.

Chances are he's still a bit pissed and that last night's imbibing will catch up with him later, but there's no time to think about that now. He dresses, brushes his hair, cleans his teeth, runs the electric shaver over his face. The stubble had been getting itchy and was looking a bit too ginger for his liking. Miraculously, he makes the bus with time to spare, before realising he's not eaten. Shit.

8:59 and he's still on the bus, stuck in traffic and some distance from work. An accident up ahead or something. His colon starts creaking and his mouth's as dry as a pro's quim. He thinks he should phone in to let his boss know he'll be late, but the battery on his phone's dead. He'd forgotten to charge it last night. The bus drops him at the office 10 minutes late. In the office, firing up his workstation, positioning his chair, the usual routine. This morning it's harder than usual though. A hangover is starting to kick in. His head's pounding and his guts are churning. And hovering at his shoulder, it's his manager. Wants a word.

Back at his desk, still bruised from his bollocking – the bus was late defence was no defence – should have got an earlier bus, was the counter, and his phone's dead battery was no excuse for not phoning in. The fact it was a mere 10-minute delay counted for nothing and it would be a written warning next time – The phone rang. He took the call, went through the scripted schpiel, dispensed some pointless information to the frustrated old goat at the other end of the line, updated the systems, shunted some papers around. Rinse and repeat. The phone rang. He took the call. Etc. Such is the daily grind of the 9-5.

Tension was building now. The hangover wasn't helping, he always got anxious when suffering the withdrawal. Slow creeping paranoia, he felt as though his boss was watching his every move to make sure he wasn't away from his desk when he shouldn't be, wasn't making personal calls or accessing the Internet for non-work purposes.

Lunchtime rolled around and he was glad of the fresh air. He didn't really feel like eating all that much, but could feel himself flagging so stocked up on crisps and chocolate for later, and purchased a can of Coke to give himself the pep he needed.

The afternoon was a drag, even more so than usual. The influx of work – phone calls, emails, paper correspondence – demanding his attention was ceaseless. 5:30 seemed a long way off. Being pulled out for a second meeting by his boss for not turning over enough calls an hour really put his back up. He tried to defend his 'stats' by pointing out that it was simply impossible to get rid of some callers, but the manager was having none of it. And the issue of his timekeeping is brought up again. A rage welled in his chest. His boss was a snotty little cunt who had no idea of what actually doing the work entailed. He was momentarily tempted to get his coat and get the fuck out there and then. But he took a piss, washed his face and calmed down and decided to stick it out till 5.30. Eventually it came, and he headed home.

His house was a shit-tip but he couldn't be arsed to do anything about it. He cracked open one of the cans left from the night before and called out for a pizza. It had been a shitty day and he deserved some kind of compensation, some kind of comfort. At least tomorrow was Friday.

6. Friday I'm in Love

Bollocks! He awoke with a start. He had been deep in sleep, in the middle of some long and winding epic dream. There had been some crazy alarms and sirens, fires everywhere and bombs dropping.... but in a jolting instant he realised that the alarm of his dream had been the alarm clock by the bed. How long ha it been going? He checks the time: 8:02. Fuck, shit, bollocks, bugger fuck cunt, he's going to have to get a move on. He hauls his arse out of bed and throws on yesterday's clothes that are strewn at the foot of the bed. No time for breakfast – he's still out of milk, and bread, too – he brushes his hair, cleans his teeth. He's running late, so no time for a shave today. 8:27 and he's having to run to make the 8:30 bus: the bus-stop is an eight and a half minute walk but he can make it in half that at a run. He hates running, because he's not fit – too much beer, too many cigarettes – and he hates arriving at work an exhausted ball of sweat. But he can't be late. He's in luck: the bus is running a couple of minutes late, and he arrives, panting and thoroughly fagged out just as it pulls up.

It doesn't take long before the tedium sets in. He usually enjoys Fridays - the vibe tended to be more upbeat, and everyone felt the tension lift as they coasted toward the weekend. But the morning dragged, and he could feel his boss' eyes on him, boring into the back of his head. He was keeping his nose clean and his head down. Same as ever, really. He couldn't fathom why this authoritarian jumpstart little prick had it in for him. Probably for no other reason than because he seemed like an easy target for the power-tripping jobsworth cunt. He tried to convince himself of this, but was certain that the fat bitch at the next desk was shooting him suspicious glances. She was a conniving manipulative cow at the best of times, and while he thought their run-in from a few weeks ago had blown over, perhaps she'd been biding her time before deciding to make him pay by using underhanded tactics. So the truth hurt, and if she couldn't take being told that she was a lazy, ass-climbing selfish lump of lard who couldn't get a shag because she was such a miserable, self-seeking boot, it was her tough shit.

The calls keep on coming, but, less frequent, he finds his concentration drifting and his time between calls clock-watching. It's payday: there are beers with his name on, and he can't wait to get stuck in!

Midday and he was close to the turtle's head so decided rushed the closing of the call he was on and go and bab one out. The humid fug of body-temperature merde hung heavy in the air, and he was dismayed to find the seat still warm. But he wasn't in a position to be picky. He laid his cable swiftly and was back at his desk within 4 minutes.

The afternoon drags, but 5:30 eventually rolls round and he's down the pub inside 5 minutes. Steve arrives, then Andy, then Simon, with Joe and Garry in tow. They're all buoyed up because it's Friday and they're raring to go. The first round is pulled and they get stuck in, it's onto round two in under 10 minutes. Ok, Varsity's not everyone's first choice, but it's close to work and it's a place to go to meet people. And, as Andy points out, there are some tidy birds in there, especially on a Friday night. The dollybirds from the offices nearby would be tottering in wearing their high heels, short skirts and low cut tops before long. He felt like trying his hand for some action tonight. He'd not had his end away in months now, and he was getting tired of the hand-shandies. He was feeling lucky, but needed to build his courage first. The totty began rolling up, right on cue and before long it was wall-to-wall minge, there for the taking. Andy got the next round in, and as the beers really start to flow, he's on his way....

7. Saturday Night's Alright (For Fighting), or, Living for the Weekend

He woke around 10. Didn't feel too bad. Probably still drunk. But he was home and in his own bed. Beat the sofa, or, worse, the gutter or a police cell. Would've been nice to have been someone else's bed, he thought, but waking up next to some eight-pint hound wouldn't've been good. The pungent aroma of the previous night's smoke which clung to his clothes, hair and skin, mingled with the sickly-sweet tartness of stale sweat made his stomach lurch, but he observed with relieve that his bed was free of puke and he'd not pissed or shat himself either.

He moaned and gingerly winched himself out of bed. Went to the bathroom, pissed like a horse for a good couple of minutes. Bliss! He ambled into the kitchen and tossed some stale bread in the toaster. Checked the clock: force of habit. He buttered the hot toast on ejection from the machine and took a couple of bites. The hangover was starting to kick in. His head's pounding and his guts are churning. He takes a heavy beershit, then gets dressed.

A trip to the supermarket takes a decent chunk out of his day. He hates going to the supermarket, but needs must, and sometimes there are some fine fillies out and about. He once pulled a bird in the supermarket. Just sidled on up to her in the cereal aisle, like in the Cornflakes ad, only smoother of course. Went out for a couple of weeks. She'd been alright to look at, but a major pain in the arse, wanted a relationship and all that shit. He wasn't up for all that, he was the free and single, wild oats type. As he's just been paid, he treats himself to a couple of frozen pizzas, stocks up on the microwave meals, a crate of Carling on special, bread, milk, bacon for a fry-up tomorrow. Throws in a pack of puddings – sundae type things – and some Smirnoff Ice, too. He might have a couple of those while warming up for tonight.

Decisions, decisions! The shorter checkout queue, or the checkout with the tasty piece serving? No contest! He threw in some smooth lines while the cute bit of fluff scanned his goods. Never mind his goods, he was checking out hers!

Once home, he flicks on the television, watches the football. Necks a couple of the cans of Carling. Throws a pizza in the oven for an early tea before it's time to start getting ready. Going out tonight, going out tonight... While the pizza was heating through, he fired up the PC and surfed for porn. A quick flog of the hog, and then, while munching on the pizza, he flitted around on Facebook and downed a couple more tins.

Turning off the computer, he docked his i-Pod and scanned for the Hard-Fi album. Cranked it up while he took a shower. Squirted a large dollop of shampoo onto his head, worked to a lather. Rinse and repeat. As seen on TV. Stepped out of the shower, towelled dry, starting with a jaunty flossing. Pumped the volume up even higher when 'Living for the Weekend' came on as he doused himself in deodorant and doused himself in aftershave. So rarely did a song sum up his life so completely. Yes, this song was his life. He fucking loved it.

Started off in Wetherspoon's, then on to Yates's. After that, a quick stop in Varsity. Ok, Varsity's not everyone's first choice, but it's a place to go to meet people. And, as Andy points out, there are some tidy birds in there, especially on a Saturday night.

The round is pulled and they get stuck in, it's onto the next in under 10 minutes. The dollybirds from the local offices, and the shop-workers too – there were some particularly tasty checkout girls in some of the supermarkets, not to mention the chicks in the clothing stores, even River Island and Top Man – would be tottering in wearing their high heels, short skirts and low cut tops before long. He felt like trying his hand for some action tonight. He'd not had his end away in months now, and he was getting tired of the hand-shandies. He was feeling lucky, but needed to build his courage first. The totty began rolling up, right on cue and before long it was wall-to-wall flange, there for the taking. Andy got the next round in, and as the beers really start to flow, he's on his way....

8. Sunday Bloody Sunday

Sunday morning. Hangover. Took him a moment to realise where he was. Home. His own bed. A good sign. Fully dressed. He glanced around, the movement of his eyeballs in their sockets making him wince in pain. The pungent aroma of the previous night's smoke which clung to his clothes, mingled with the sickly-sweet tartness of stale sweat made his stomach lurch, but he observed with relieve that his bed was free of puke and he'd not pissed or shat himself either. Ok, so it was rare for either of those things to happen, but they weren't unheard of. How had he got home? And when? Where had he been, even? After arriving at the club, already hammered, some time after ten or thereabouts, everything was a blank. He felt like shit, felt like he was gonna die.

He moaned and gingerly winched himself out of bed. Went to the bathroom, pissed like a horse for a good couple of minutes. Bliss! Chugged half a pint of full-fat milk straight from the carton, threw down some painkillers and tossed some bread in the toaster. Checked the clock. Ok, so it wasn't Sunday morning any more, it was closer to 1pm. A seriously heavy night. He buttered the hot toast on ejection from the machine and took a couple of bites before a wave of nausea broke from the pit of his stomach. He made haste back to the bathroom and spewed it all back up. Mouth, nose, some serious velocity. He wiped his mouth with the back of his hand and crawled back to bed.

The next time he woke it was just after 3pm. He still felt rough, but nothing like the way he had felt before. What a waste of a day. Still in the clothes from the night before, he went back to the kitchen and prepared a mammoth fried breakfast and sat in front of the television while he troughed down the greasy collation. There was a match on. He didn't really give a shit about Liverpool or Chelsea, being a Man U supporter but football's football.

Afternoon rolled into evening as he sat, vegetating, on the sofa. Fuck it, he couldn't be arsed to wash up or so any washing, not today. It would keep. Around 8, he decided to take a shower, after which, still wrapped in his towel, he fired up the PC and checked his emails. Nothing much doing. He logged into his Facebook account. A few tagged pics from last night were up already, and a number of people had left him comments, too. But as far as he could ascertain, he'd only danced like a twat and tried cracking onto a couple of birds, both absolute munters, by all accounts. But he'd not screwed either of them – because they'd turned him down flat – and he'd not flashed his cock or arse, so on balance, no cause for concern. He idly flipped up some porn pages. Before long, his horn was throbbing as hard as his head had been earlier in the day, and he knocked out a mix over a couple of chicks lezzing it up. Job done, he wiped himself down, put the telly on and watched some second-rate eighties action movie till just gone midnight. Waste of a day, alright, but it sure as hell beat having to go to work.

Afterhours

Some nights it's just impossible to sleep. And sleep is like exercise: the less you do, the less you're capable of. Creeping insomnia, starts with a bad night or two where it's hard to get off, hard to switch off, hard to get comfortable, hard to forget. At what point does a late night become an early morning, becomes not worth going to bed? Before you know it, you've lost so much sleep that you forget how to sleep...

I forget how it started. By 'it,' I mean this particular bout of insomnia. The true origins of my suffering from sleeplessness go back a long way and are now lost in the mists of time. But this particular spell has been perhaps the worst yet. I must have had something or another on my mind. Money, work, something. Or perhaps I'd simply had too much caffeine or excitement and got carried away with playing computer games, reading or surfing the net because I didn't feel especially tired and consequently lost track of time. It's easily done. Especially in the summer months, when it's light until the small hours and in reality never gets properly dark.

Time was when I used to be scared of being awake late into the night. I remember lying awake as a child, my unease building. The later it became, the more agitated I would become. I would go downstairs and complain to my parents that I couldn't sleep. They would pack me back off to bed with a warm drink or advice to think calming thoughts, imagining myself by a tranquil lakeside or somesuch. None of these things ever worked. Sometimes they would suggest I read, and that would make me sleepy. But reading never made me sleepy: whatever I read, be it a book or, less commonly, a comic, the reading matter would simply stir more thoughts that would stimulate rather than relax me. But more often than not, as the clock on my bedside ticked the seconds and minutes past, my awareness of the passing time and the growing lateness would build, and before long I would be too busy focusing on the fact I was still awake to concentrate on the act of reading.

It wasn't that I was scared of the dark: no, I was simply scared of being the only one left awake. Perhaps it was a fear of being alone. But I remember hearing my parents getting ready for bed and the panic rising. I would hear the landing light go off and the fear would begin to take hold. For a short while I would hear the rumble of their voices and, straining my eyes, I would be able to just make out – or so I believed – the faint light escaping from the crack in the doorway to their bedroom. Then everything would fall silent, and finally, the last flake of light would be extinguished. I was alone, in the dark. The only sounds I could hear were my own breathing and the roar of my circulating blood in my ears. No, wait, I could hear my own heartbeat, too, and of course the rustle of my bedding as I tossed and turned and turned and tossed in my panic-stricken but futile attempts to get comfortable and, ultimately, to sleep.

Things changed during my adolescence. I learned to embrace my insomnia. I got a television in my room. I soon discovered that late-night television was often much more exciting than daytime television, and where it wasn't more exciting, it was certainly more unusual, more esoteric. The advent of 24-hour television saved my life. Or something. It certainly stopped me from being scared or being awake at night. Instead of trying to sleep, I turned my head around and made every effort to stay awake, watching strange films on Channel 4 and Open University programmes on BBC2. The Gulf War in 1991 was something else. Real live war action! Sometimes if I close my eyes I can still see those green comet tails of missiles in the black sky. I can still revisualise the fluorescence of the explosions as the missiles hit their targets. The footage was grainy, fuzzy, shot in night-vision from long-range, but it was like nothing I'd seen before. I was watching it, live, as it happened, these images being beamed directly into my room and burning themselves onto my corneas. This was my moon landing. This was the revolution, and it *was* being televised! I would of course grow weary eventually, and turn off the television and immediately fall sleep around 2 or 3am.

These recollections aren't entirely representative, of course. I have gone for months, even years, without having any difficulties sleeping. And even when my sleep patterns have become disturbed, I have always maintained a 'normal' life: that is to say, I didn't allow myself to become nocturnal, or even the sort to lead the classic student lifestyle, lying in bed until midday, even on weekends. In fact, quite the contrary: I've always been one for getting up in the mornings, getting up and getting on with things, and if I've not gone to bed until 4 or 5am, I'll still be up between 6 and 7 on most days. Life's too short to spend it in bed asleep. There's always something to do, something to see; life never stops.

But recently things have been particularly bad. There's no escape. None of my problems is, in itself, so significant. A late bill here and there, a misunderstanding between friends. The bank statement arrives and shows a greater deficit than expected. Panic rises: how will I eat now? How will I pay that credit card bill? A relationship turns sour, a bad day at the office. All manageable on their own, a small personal crisis, nothing but a second-division fret, is a league away from a breakdown. But you know how it is; a plethora of minor stresses and niggles conglomerate, and collectively they conspire to build into a maze of dead-ends, growing like ivy on a dying tree. It's impossible to determine which entwined creeping tendril begins where, there's no way to unravel the individual trails, to differentiate one from another as they meld together to form a solid mat of damp-coated, insect-ridden fronds. The creeping forest floor becomes your life and there's no seeing the wood for the trees. You go to work but can't concentrate. You go home and can't eat. You go out but can't communicate. You return home but can't sleep.

Realising that a new cycle of sleeplessness was in the ascendancy, I changed my routine and gave up getting ready for bed at 11pm and instead began to find activities that would occupy my time, perhaps even distract me, in the hope that physical fatigue would, before long, overrule my mental activity and enable me to sleep. I played guitar for hours, strumming all the tunes I had learned, teaching myself new tunes, even writing new ones. Once my fingers were too sore to play any more, I would change my activity, either listening to CDs I hadn't played in years and reel dizzily as the memories flooded back, or reading a book or magazine. All too often, though, I would find myself either on-line or watching mindrot late-night television. Whatever I did, the outcome was the same.

It's been ongoing for weeks now. I have no idea how I'm managing to function. I'm walking through life on empty. I'm on autopilot. I go to work but can't concentrate. I go home and am unable to eat. I've been out a few times, got drunk, stated sober, it's all the same, I can't communicate. I return home and I'm dead on my feet but still can't sleep. I sit. I watch the hours go by. I live another life. This isn't me. I look in the mirror and don't know whose face it is looking back at me. I'm not here anymore. But life goes on.

Tonight, however, was different. I'd taken a few days off work; I had holiday to burn and didn't really feel that my being there in my present state was of any real benefit to anyone. Today was Wednesday, but I spent the day like a Saturday. I went to the supermarket and bought some food, all budget crap but all I can afford. The day drifted by, and before long the day was done. The sun slowly trickled down behind the roofs leaving a smear of blood and mascara where it slid down the sky. 10pm rolled by. I could hear the volume of traffic on the main road a couple of streets away had dropped off. Eleven o' clock.... tick, tock.... the sound of voices came and went as groups of people, mostly students,

returning from the pubs passed on their way home. Watching the clock now...
two minutes to midnight.... one... Midnight hit and the voices had stopped, as
had the traffic save for the occasional lone vehicle. 1 o' clock jump, and all was
silent. 2 o' clock in the morning, 94 degrees... England fades away.

I got wired... I began to get frightened, not for fear of the dark or of
being alone, the last one awake as I had as a child, but, unable to embrace the
insomnia as I had previously, I began to feel a creeping dread, a fear at the lack of
control, my inability to break out of the grip of terminal wakefulness. With no
company save for the television, the radio, the Internet, my CD collection, a few
books and magazines, I began to feel caged, hemmed... with the aforementioned
sources having been the sole input into my life over the last few days, things
began to blur, bend and blend in the most unpredictable of ways... Words and
phrases entered my head completely at random. I was unable to recall from when
they came. Had I heard it on the television, or on the radio? Was it something
someone had said to me once, either a few weeks ago, or many years in the
anterior? Had I overheard it in the shop while queuing to buy milk? Or had I
read it in a book? Was it dialogue, or perhaps even a line from a song? Confusion
reigned as I very rapidly lost touch with everything, including myself. Baffled and
scared by life itself, I truly knew not whether I was coming or going, what day of
the week it was, or indeed, whether it was day or night. Instead of watching the
television for entertainment or even company I realised I was beginning to
simply exist as a sponge, not so much the antennae of the race but the black hole
at the centre of nothing a void in the desert of time... I wasn't simply listening to
those records of reading those books, I was becoming them. Or, more accurately,
perhaps, they were becoming me, as my personality ebbed from me, to be
replaced through some bizarre process of absorption or osmosis, by everything
that circulated about me. 3am: eternal. Clocks stopped. A grinding halt. Nothing
moved. Time in slow motion, a second dragged out to an hour.

4am rolls around and I have to do something. I need to break out of this
prison. It was time to face the night head on Outside, the night has submerged
everything in darkness, chill and silent. Winter is fully embedded now, and the air
is cold. Despite the low temperature that bites my fingers, ears and the tip of my
nose, my breath makes no vapour, so dry is the atmosphere. The sky is
surprisingly clear. Living on the outskirts of the city, I wander the residential
streets of the suburbs close to my home. The light pollution is minimal, and
looking up I am surprised by just how many stars I can actually see. The moon
looms large and silvery. I am also surprised, as I pass the houses, just how many
people still seem to be up. although most are in darkness, there are still some
lights on. Why are they up? post-clubbers? Night-shifters? Early starters? Or
chronic insomniacs like me? I move through the night, the cover of darkness my
cloak of invisibility. Glancing toward the illuminated rectangles as I pass, I
cannot help but look, and in some I am able to see the outlines of figures moving
inside, moving silhouettes, people's actions projected like life-size shadow-
puppetry. Some have not even closed their curtains, and I can see into their living

rooms and bedrooms. I feet nothing, a complete detachment. It doesn't feel wrong. I don't feel nosey. I don't feel as though I am in any way spying into their homes or voyeuristically peeping into their private lives. Separated by the glass and the distance and the still, dead air, cold and silent, it's like watching television on mute. My presence goes unnoticed as they play out their parts. I am simply a viewer, not participating or interacting in any way. Here, now, I realise something is different. I feel calm. I draw the fresh cold air deep into my lungs, and feel as though a weight is lifting from me. I bury my hands deep in my pockets and smile to myself as I turn around and head home. I feel good. I am finally ready to sleep again.

Get a Little Bit Closer: Memoir, Accessibility and Brushing Virtual Shoulders with Celebrity

This is something that's seemingly crept up on me while I've been immersed in various writing projects and pouring over lyric books and websites while researching a story of indeterminate length I'm currently working on (just in case anyone thought I may have been dwelling in a cultural vacuum with no access to television or internet with my eyes closed and my fingers in my ears), because until recently I was largely unaware of the popularity of memoir and, equally, the accessibilising (yes, I'm coining a new term) of celebrities. Perhaps that's simply because although I like to think I have a reasonable idea of what's going on in the mainstream, I nevertheless tend to focus my energies on things that interest me. Really, life's too short to squander too much time on bad books, bad music, crap blockbusters and even crapper television programmes. Which means that while I will drop in on Big Brother every now and again, I'm not wired to the box 24/7 for the 3 months or whatever it's on for.

Now, I already knew that biographies (and crummy autobiographies ghosted for retard pseudo-celebrities who've done precisely fuck all in their short overprivileged lives) have topped the best seller lists for some years now, and that the proliferation of bollocks magazines like OK! Grazia, etc., etc., ad nauseam, all filled with grainy paparazzi shots of sagging tits and bad cellulite is more than evidence of our obsession with 'celebrity' and also with propagating the all-too-obvious fact that all that separates these figures of international renown is, in essence, a bank balance and a publicist. Yes, your favourite celebrity, for all their fame and wealth, has a spare tyre just like you, gets pissed and looks like crap at 2 in the morning just like you... you get the idea. As if it takes a genius to fathom that they are, after all, only human. But non-celebrity memior..?

What really surprised me was the discovery I made when leafing through the sleeve notes to the Strapping Young lad album 'Alien' that a friend of mine had lent me. No, the fact that I was disappointed by their appearance wasn't the surprise, and nor was the fact that I was disappointed by the music, which isn't a patch on the albums I already have, 'City' and 'Heavy as a Really Heavy Thing' – the reason for this being that the band appear to have slumped from making a wall-of-noise industrial strength racket to fairly MOR nu-metal fare, replete with wanky solos (you can't blame it all on the production). What struck me was the page of credits. A paragraph of credits for each musician. No, I didn't bother to read them all. It was the principal. Ok, so all bands have some assistance in the recording of their albums, all bands use amps and other equipment and have preferred brands of gear, all bands have friends and family and fans and managers and roadies and groupies and engineers and bands they've played with, bands they're influenced by, blah blah blah. We don't need to know about it. And thanking your mum's ok if it's your first record and you're a 15 year old kid in a wet, drippy indie band, but for hairy, hoary old rockers to do it is fucking tragic. I for one prefer to think of my hairy, hoary rock idols as having been spawned, or grown like mould on a slice of bread in the dank bowels of hell rather than having parents. And certainly not mothers they love and go round for Sunday dinner with. It's just not rock 'n' roll, man. But it seems that this is emblematic of a wider issue, regarding the way that people – individuals, artists bands, whoever – present themselves a lot more openly now, a point I've touched on previously when discussing the lack of restraint some people seem to have when sharing everything – and I mean everything – with the world and his dog via their blogs.

This also set me thinking about the way we perceive bands more generally. Specifically, it set me thinking about the way I perceive bands more generally. Of course, as one grows older, one's perception changes somewhat. Some of that has to do with a growing awareness of the process – the one whereby a band records an album puts out a single some time ahead as a taster, to create a buzz, and then another one a couple of weeks before or after the album, does a round of promotional interviews, a tour, put out another single (often using live tracks recorded on the tour to save having to record any additional b-sides and maybe to help plug the previous album) then go off and work on the next album. Rinse and repeat, every couple of years or so. Of course there are exceptions to the rule and some occasional deviations from and variations on the pattern, but that's the general framework. I'm not sure precisely when I became aware of the 'rules' – probably in my early teens, when I started collecting records properly, and buying new singles and albums in the week, or even on the day – of release. Partly out of a fear of the limited edition selling out, and partly through excitement and anticipation. And having a rather obsessive streak. But with that kind of knowledge, a certain degree of mystery is lost. Up to the dawning of that awareness, songs got into the charts, were played on the radio – I always listened to the Top 40 on Radio 1 and watched 'Top of the Pops' – and they'd be around for a while and you could go to Woolworths or WHS and pick them up a while later. I had no idea about *the process*.

Things are very different now, of course. Airplay starts about 2 months before a single release, it makes a stratospheric entry into the charts – or fails to chart despite being a release by a big-name band – then plummets off the radar. If you don't buy a single within a week or two of release – unless it's one of those that lingers in the charts for fucking months – you'll struggle to find it. And you'll not get it in Woolworths because they're ceasing the sale of CD singles this year. I haven't been into WHS in about a decade because they stocked nothing of interest to me once I had discovered that my tastes were less mainstream where music – and books – is concerned. Even albums, apart from the big-selling and standard titles become more difficult to find in high street stores like HMV after a not-so-long time. This only serves to accentuate just how driven by marketing formulae the industry is.

It's perhaps less of an issue with smaller bands, and bands that are on the kind of labels that simply can't operate in keeping with the commercial model. Some bands and labels are practically cottage industries. This again reflects the nature of our contemporary society, as characterised by, simultaneously, an immense homogenisation of culture as represented by the mainstream, and an extreme fragmentation, as represented by anything outside the mainstream. While the mainstream becomes increasingly centred around mass-production – which seems to run contra to the public's craving for greater access, the non-mainstream relies on a closer relationship between the artist and the fan. In order to promote their work, the band – or writer, or whoever – is required to get out there and do it themselves. But perhaps this isn't such a contradiction: the more famous (i.e. mainstream) the celebrity, the more access the public wants. And because direct interaction simply isn't feasible, it has to be made through social networking and through guts-on-display biography and memoir.

I also believe that new bands often have a certain enigma, which soon fades. The trick is to maintain a degree of mystery. But so few succeed in doing so, and it's at that point that some – much – of the magic is lost. Hearing a song for the first time, one can wonder who the band, what they look like. But television and magazine interviews can very quickly spoil things, when you learn that they're a bunch of trendies with nothing to say for themselves. And they only have the one song that's any good. You feel cheated.

So, returning to my central point, namely the accessiblisation of celebrities, there's little doubt in my mind that the Internet, and particularly networking sites such as MySpace, has had a profound effect on the trend toward this accessibility. The celebrity has a blog. The fans can read it, and can comment on it, directly, immediately. It's a lot closer in communication terms than the old fan-mail which may earn a mass-produced signed photo by way of a response. Indeed, MySpace even promote their featured 'celebrities' with the lead 'get closer to...' But is it so desirable to do so? For a start, there's nothing worse than meeting one of your heroes only to discover that they're a complete twat. It spoils everything and it's impossible to view their work in the same way ever again. And discovering a noisy rock band are a bunch of mummy's boys is just as bad. And many writers and musicians are quite shy, retiring, private types. Moreover, many writers will almost inevitably use autobiographical elements within their fiction, and that's as much as they're wanting to give away. What's so wrong with that?

I'm not suggesting that such interaction in any way encourages stalking, probably quite the contrary (after all, there's less 'need' if it's all out there). But it does indubitably alter the relationship between the artist and the fan. There's now a certain expectation for the artist – or celebrity – to put it all out there in public. But how much information do we need? I'm all for the demystification of the creative process in the way Burroughs did with the cut-ups, for example. But a little bit of mystery goes a long way. Yes, it's perhaps unhealthy to place 'celebrities' and artists (in whatever medium) on pedestals and the acceptance that they are human and fallible is important. They may be special, but they're not deities. Treating them as such isn't good for anyone. Diva syndrome's not pretty or conducive to the creative process. So, whatever the prevailing obsession with celebrity dirty laundry and lifestyle may be, sometimes, less really is more and yes, you really can have too much of a good thing.

Candidate

It was just another day at the office, the same as any other. Ben sat at his desk. He had spent the last three hours trying desperately to compile his latest report based on a series of site visits to out-of-town shopping developments ahead of Friday's deadline, but it was proving nigh on impossible. For a start, the buildings were in a poor state of repair: his surveys had uncovered a number of significant structural flaws which were bad news all round. The trouble was, he found these modern prefabricated monstrosities composed of concrete and corrugated iron the most uninspiring of all buildings to assess, and while he had most of the information he required to hand, some of his notes were a little patchy regarding some of the sites, as he had been tired, bored and hungover while conducting the surveys. That said, he didn't really find buildings in themselves all that inspiring. Surveying hadn't been a calling for him, but then, for whom is surveying a calling, a passion? Surveying was a job, which required an even and pragmatic approach to factual data and a grasp of figures and certain scientific concepts regarding the deterioration of concrete, the weakening of iron girders, the flammability of certain materials and so on. The appreciation of architecture was not a prerequisite for becoming a surveyor of commercial property. But the modern out-of-town retail park developments were still the worst: once you had seen one, you had seen them all. But feeling tired and grotty made any report on such buildings even more wearisome, and with a tight deadline looming, even more troublesome to a man who was not a big fan of typing long reports, preferring, if possible, to keep communications down to brief notes and bullet-points. Equally troublesome, his phones – landline and mobile – kept ringing, interfering with his train of though. No sooner had he regained his flow and begun formulating a coherent sentence detailing the defects in the roofing structures or damp coursing than another call would demand his attention and haul him away from the job at hand for just long enough for him to forget exactly what it was he had been about to write next.

Ben sat and rubbed his eyes with his thumb and forefinger. His skin felt rough and dry, his eyes sensitive and watery. He was exhausted, and this was reflected in his sallow appearance. He had spent the last week and a half driving long-distance between the sites he was surveying for this report – Wednesday last, Sheffield, Thursday last Birmingham, Friday last Nottingham, followed by Bath on Monday, Stoke on Tuesday, Newcastle on Wednesday and Norwich this morning – before returning to the office with a sheaf of scribbled notes, digital camera shots, notes recorded on a Dictaphone while on the tops of various buildings, muffled and inaudible due to high winds blasting across the mic as he had mumbled tiredly and unenthusiastically about various joists and joints. He rubbed his eyes again and returned his bleary eyes to the screen.

The Foo Fighters' track 'The Best of You' rattled from his pocket for the umpteenth time that day. He loved that song – it rocked – but he was beginning to tire of its polyphonic yet stunted ring-tone version intruding into his life every five minutes. He checked the name on the incoming call. It was Ruth, his 'better half.' They had been together almost eight years now – long enough for him to have known almost instinctively that it would have been her ringing this time.

"Hi, Ru," he said, half sighing, half croaking, his voice cracked with fatigue.

"Hey," she chirruped back.

A slight pause – as was customary. He never liked to jump in and ask why she was phoning this time – it sounded tetchy, and she was the sensitive type – but she never came straight out with anything either, hence the waggledance of telephonic etiquette each time they spoke, even after this time. Particularly after this time: it has become habit, and he knew it. He knew not, however, of a way to break it, or even if there was any point in doing so – or even if he wanted to do so. It was harmless, but did take seconds out of his busy day. Seconds that could have been spent on other matters. He fought this involuntary irritation that he felt – that he had been feeling for the past few weeks, or possibly longer, he's not been paying that much attention as he'd had a lot going on – and reminded himself that Ruth didn't actually do anything to annoy him and that his tiredness was simply making him irrationally irritable. It wasn't his fault he was tired and stressed. It wasn't her fault he was tired and stressed. He just was.

"Hey," he echoed back, as he commonly did. It bought time, breathing space, signalled to her that he was listening, like a call-and-response of 'Copy,' 'Roger.'

"I was just wondering what time you'd be home for tea tonight," she said in her usual even, gentle tone.

He sighed and rubbed his tired, itchy eyes again. Ruth liked her routine. Daily, she called around 3.30 or 4pm to enquire when he'd be home, although he was rarely able to give a specific answer. There were invariably deadlines to be met, which frequently entailed working later than anticipated, however he budgeted his time, however hard he worked, and however closely he worked to the premise that however long one anticipates something taking, double it and add ten per cent to get a more accurate estimate. Then there was the matter of the drive home. On a good day – or a weekend – it would be a 40-minute drive. But on a weekday, during the rush two hours, it could be anything up to an hour and a half, and that was provided there were no accidents, freak storms or other unusual circumstances which may extend the journey time still further.

"I dunno," he replied after a pause. "I've got a lot on at the moment."

"Ok, do you think you'll be home before eight-ahuh?" she asked, her voice rising at the end and a small not-quite-laugh following the last syllable. He pictured her, smiling as she did, her nose wrinkled a little and her eyes half-closed, an endearing expression which he had been fond of from the outset when they had met some seven years ago. How time flew! He had been in his early twenties then, and having recently relocated following the securing of a decent job in Leeds, Ben had been on the brink of embarkation on his career proper.

"I don't know," he reiterated. "I hope so, but I wouldn't like to say for definite."

"Ok, well I thought we might have chops tonight and they grill in no time, so I shall wait until you get in before starting the tea."

"Fine."

"Call me when you're leaving work?"

"Sure."

"Ok, I'll speak to you later, bye."

"Yeah, bye."

He couldn't help it, he knew he sounded 'off.' The simple fact was that he had been feeling decidedly fractious lately, and it was difficult to pinpoint the exact reasons why. And because he didn't know, he felt he couldn't really talk about it with Ruth – what was there to say? It was his problem, and he didn't want to push it onto her. She had her own things going on, namely the fact that she would soon be unemployed – again. After a succession of unappealing and unsatisfactory temporary jobs, mostly in big corporate offices, the type of place she hated – so many people, so many awful people, the sort she'd not have given a moment of her time to through choice – she had landed herself a fantastic job on a museum archiving project. Only now the project was almost done and the funding had run dry and so her contract was to be terminated in a couple of weeks. Ruth's unemployment, or otherwise low wages did place a strain on things for them financially. Again, Ben never liked to make an issue of it, because to do so would be unfair. He accepted, and in some ways, thrived on fulfilling his role as the dominant male, the breadwinner. He'd always been ambitious, and while he'd never been certain as to what career he wished to pursue, he'd always been ambitious to earn. A good income, a nice house, a fast car…. It's what every man wants, and it had always been his dream to live the life, to work hard and to reap the rewards, and to spend those rewards in such a way that everyone who saw him knew it, that he was a successful person.

But right now he didn't feel successful, and he was struggling to put his finger on exactly what the root of his niggling discontent was. But he had realised that he was not content, and despite his reasonable income - £42K pa plus car plus mobile phone, etc., was a fair salary, he knew that, although after tax there was little benefit, he felt, to earning £42K over earning £25K. He knew he wasn't like those he left behind in school, those whose profiles he had read on Friends Reunited….

HI TO ALL THAT REMEMBER ME!!! STILL LIVING IN LINCOLN...HAVE A SON AND A DAUGHTER ...LIVING WITH MY PARTNER, RICKY, AND VERY HAPPY AND SETTLED...DONE SEVERAL DIFFERENT JOBS...INCLUDING CHILDCARE AND RETAIL...AND MORE RECENTLY POOL MAINTENANCE...

Im married to Gareth Homes who's still sexy and gorgeous and a builder Phwarrah. I work with homeless and vulnerable young people. No kids HURRAY! But got four dogs.

hi, I got married nearly five years ago i have three lovely sons bradyn is nearly 6 rio is 3 and flynn is 2, Just moved to norfolk after living in Germany for the past three years.

I am now job hopping in sales and marketing in norfolk i have a little boy named ben
born in 2003 and another on the way living life to the max

Perhaps that's part of the problem, Ben had mused as he had read that final entry posted by some no-mark loser he did not even so much as vaguely recall from school. He did wonder if perhaps he wasn't 'living life to the max.' He didn't exactly feel as though he was. But then, what exactly does living life to the max entail? Certainly not doing sales and marketing in Norfolk….

He was better than them and he knew it. And yet, somehow, somewhere in his mind he envied them as much as he loathed despised them. They were sad, they were pathetic, they were going nowhere, they had achieved nothing, would never achieve anything, earn anything like the salary he was already commanding. To earn more, however, would require an awful lot of graft, and would certainly require some difficult decision-making with regard to his work/life balance, and possibly even place further strain on his relationship.

He rubbed is eyes again. Checked his watch again. Looked at the screen. He had made next to no progress during the last three hours and he could feel his frustration building.

"Sod it," he muttered under his breath.

He opened his wallet and checked the contents. Three ten pound notes and a scraggy fiver. There were regular trains home if required. He turned off the computer. There was only one thing for it... get roaring drunk. He'd drink himself into oblivion. A short term solution, perhaps. But things would look a whole lot better tomorrow.

The Fear

Wait, stay calm. Tries to control his breathing; he's shaking. Can't silence the roar of blood like the ocean at Spring tide in his ears. Burning up – he's on fire. Dizzy. Trembling. Light-headed. Vision blurred. Clammy palms, sticky fingers. Fists clenched, white knuckles. He's afraid, so afraid. These physiological symptoms only accentuate this all-consuming sense of terror. Panting like a dog. Lack of oxygen, like the air's been sucked thin by some invisible force. These are new sensations. He had always felt as though he had been in control – until recently.

35 and he's at a crossroads. He had never really given the future all that much consideration. But now his pat stretched out behind him like streaming endless ribbons; roads without beginning or end, asphalt bands disappearing into the dark horizon of lost history, and the future is well out of hand. *This isn't supposed to be how it is, this isn't what life is supposed to be like.* He didn't want to admit his confusion and fear. Fear of what precisely? A fear of fear... there's a wasted life for every day that passes, yet here he is, simply killing time.

Never certain of what he wanted, he was now certain of just one thing: that this is not what he wants. He is leaving some day. Someday never comes. Shuffles more papers around his characterless veneer desk, one in a long line of characterless veneer desks in this characterless office. A sea of dead and empty faces surrounds him. This is hell, death with walls. Falling into this job had been so easy, like falling into a pile of cushions, easy, painless, but then immediately it had become like falling endlessly as in a dream, spiralling inexorably downward, helpless in the darkness, expecting – hoping – initially at least – that the bottom would be near and would afford a soft landing and an easy, obvious exit. But as time wore on and the fall continued, hope faded along with the light above, so far away now, disappearing to a pin-prick at the top of the abyss, soon to be swallowed by the eternal void.

It would only be for a few months, he had told himself, time to build experience and to find his feet. Time to settle his finances and devise a more concrete long-term plan. To consider the options, to approach his future strategically, and to apply for ways out from a more secure position. But plans

31

can go wrong. The best laid plans and all that. That had been seven years ago. A year had elapsed and he had not given a moment's thought to the future, beyond the vague notion of 'some day.' But someday never comes. Two years, three, and he was in a rut. Colleagues came and went. More empty faces and hollow smiles from names he would forget more quickly than he would learn them, as quickly as they would appear and disappear, just passing through. When would he pass through?

It was all too easy to get sucked in and to forget about life when on the conveyor-belt of clocking on and clocking off, the endless stream of papers for stamping and stapling, filing, dispatch and disposal.

He had heard stories of employees who had snapped, gone crazy, running screaming and swearing down the aisles, thrown sheaves of confidential documents out of the window, raining down like tickertape on the streets below to the confusion and astonishment of the passers-by. He'd even heard of there having been a jumper once. Ended up as pavement-pizza, but astoundingly still alive, now simply existing in a semi-vegetable state, a crippled slobbering mess, physically and mentally incapacitated for the remainder of his sorry life. No control.

He could not understand such wayward, destructive acts, so lacking in rationale, reason or dignity, much less respect them. Breaking loose, letting go, what could it achieve? Truly, in the long term, no good could come of it: only pain, anguish and humiliation. Humiliation is a disease. To crack like that was, after all, to admit failure, surely. And failure was beyond the spectrum of his vocabulary, his sphere of comprehension. He was determined to never allow himself to taste the bitter tang of failure, yet, simultaneous to his self-made and private avowal, he was also aware that he was not a success. Yet. He was destined for more, of this he was convinced. For now, though, he would have to bide his time: endure.

Cosseted by the stability of the 9-5, life was at least bearable, tolerable on a day-to-day basis. No alarms and no surprises. The office existed as a security blanket of towering breeze-blocks, girders, concrete slabs, glass plates and mile after mile of cables and pipes that created the manmade intestines of the labyrinthine corridors of power. The staff, the worker ants, were the capillaries, while the invisible networks carried the corporation's real life-blood, its vast quantities of stored information, between the lesser organs, the servers and terminals. Somewhere, invisible, hidden away from all, was the pulsating heart of the organisation. Its identity was a mystery, perhaps even a myth, much like the fundamental purpose of the corporation itself. Was it, like a virus whose sole purpose is to replicate itself, simply to make money through the movement of information? It didn't do to question. So better to just shut your mouth.

But as he sat at his workstation, the humdrum of his familiar surroundings suddenly struck him as unnatural. The proximity to perfect strangers forced together simply by virtue of but one common feature of their uniformly sad and undistinguished lives, namely their employment, felt forced and desperate. This enclosed alienation, accentuated by the melding of man to machine, was death with walls. It made his head swim. Reeling, he felt entirely at a loss, spinning, drowning in an eternal vortex. He scanned, foe the umpteenth time, the report before him on he flat-screen VDU. Try as he might, it was proving impossible to unravel the central points, to boil it down to something meaningful. Where was it going? In that instant, the report on screen became emblematic of life itself – meandering, pointless, meaningless, directionless, futile. A distant noise; the subtle whiff of decay. The air was growing stagnant. The fear was rising once more.

The length and breadth of the office floor, clerical staff went anonymously about their anonymous business of conducting business for the business, a business for which they cared for not one iota on a personal level, so far removed were they from the company's true objectives – whatever they were. Pen-pushing of this nature was only ever a means to an end for the nameless number-crunchers, the chairpounding proletariat. Dead-end street. There were only two options, going forward: pass through quickly or become a part of the furniture. Either way, no-one paid anyone else any real attention, there was no real sense of community. Occasionally there were whispers, so-and-so unheard of from accounts had been caught *in flagrante delicto,* with their trousers down – literally – with so-and-so, also unheard of from service support on the desk of such-and-such a manager, identifiable perhaps by name but never by face. Feuds between colleagues that came to a head on departmental nights out, team-building trips or at Christmas parties also occasionally circulated via the rumour-mill, but most of it was largely meaningless, and none of it ever really amounted to anything. Such mild distractions provided a break from the monotony for the majority of the lifetime factotums who populated the open-plan spaces, but in truth only perpetuated the eternity and turgid blankness of such gainless, thankless employ. The fact remained that ultimately everyone existed within their own solipsistic little bubble and would rapidly retreat like hermit crabs when faced by a prowling predator if they had dared to venture beyond their regulated confines even momentarily.

Where was his life headed? Seven long years... and what, precisely, was the sum of hid achievements? He was no armchair philosopher – he hadn't time for such trivia or such vague conceptual thinking, and preferred to remain wholly grounded in the realities of the concrete world – but in his occasional moments of introspection, those few and fleeting quiet times, he could not help but feel somehow cheated by life. Such long and circuitous routes to arrive at more or less the same place as one started... was it worth the grief? The beginning is also the end. He rubbed his eyes with his thumb and forefinger. His skin felt rough and dry, his eyes sensitive and watery. But at least his breathing was coming more easily now, his palpitations abated, replaced by a more regular, if piston-like rhythm. He was able to focus on his screen once more. The telephone rang. Back to life, back to reality, back to business as usual.

How to Get Ahead in Business

As I see it, the corporate world, the world of business, is not life. It's work. And while a lot of people invest a lot of time in their jobs – either because they have some kind of career-driven aspirations to 'make it' in their chosen profession, or because they crave money and power, which can be obtained by climbing the corporate ladder – work is not life. Maybe for some it is, but unless you're fortunate enough to have a job that is also a hobby, something creative, or a true calling or vocation – like writing, art, sport, whatever – then the chances are quite high that you work in an office, and if that's the case and your work is your life, there's something seriously deficient. I believe 'sad cunt' is the phrase I'm clawing for here.

Me, I'm not fiscally-motivated. Moreover, while I do hold down an office job on a part-time basis (because the writing – what I consider to be my 'real' job – doesn't, at least at the present time, pay, and I'm not so willing to suffer for my art as to live on the streets and never eat), I don't really engage too deeply in the corporate philosophy, and I certainly don't subscribe to it. And so I find myself in a position that's different from most of my colleagues and friends, who work full-time (although, arguably, with my writing and so on, I probably put in more hours during the course of a week than many of them), in that I live much of my life apart from the office environment. This being apart enables me to 'enjoy' the distance to observe and reflect without being too close. I don't really invest much of myself in office politics, etc. I turn up, do my seven hours of chairpounding and then get the hell out sharp so I can crack open a beer and start typing.

Perhaps I digress. The point is that the office I a strange and unnatural environment, which is different from the real world. Not only does it present a strange fucked-up microcosm that exists parallel to the broader society, but it has its own set of rules, ethics, and, perhaps most curiously, its own language. This means you can easily identify a career corporate tosser on a train or in the street even when they're not wearing a suit (although the chances are that the suit and tie is the outfit of choice even for going to the pub or the supermarket, and the briefcase or laptop bag will be welded to the hand in a white-knuckle grip even on a journey to the corner shop), because they'll be talking loudly, either to a colleague in person or on their mobile, in what sounds like some sort of code.

Which is more or less precisely what they're doing. Here's a brief guide to come classic contemporary corporate speak.

Going Forward...

Of all of the phrases that are pointless, meaningless and overused, 'going forward' really is the highest ranker. Initially, it came in as a substitute for 'in the future,' referring to plans to progress projects, etc. Of course, it's not really about going forward in any sense other than chronologically, because much corporate activity is about dressing up the same carp to look different. Never mind the fact it still exudes the same aroma of fish. Why 'going forward' has gained such popularity is beyond me. Why not say 'in the future' which has the same number of syllables, or something meaningful dependent on the context its being used? Time was when context mattered. But going forward has gone viral. It's become the 'erm' of the corporate world. It's a phrase, a sentence and a full stop in itself. "We'll book a telecon to discuss it going forward." "Yeah, book me in on my diary going forward." As such, it's become a cliché. More than that, its ubiquitous use has stripped it of any meaning. Having heard the phrase used in interviews on the news recently, it appears that 'going forward' has actually seeped into the real world.

Reinventing the Wheel

Reinventing the wheel is something that no sensible person would attempt. And most corporate bods are sensible enough to realise this. And not reinventing the wheel is something you'll find managers bragging about. It's a new approach, but they're not trying to reinvent the wheel. Having said that....

Avoid Fillers

People pause and hesitate in conversation all the time. Sometimes it's because they're struggling for the right word. Sometimes it's simply out of habit. In linguistics, vocalised hesitations are referred to as 'fillers.' According to Michael Larcombe writing in *New Scientist* in 1995, 'silence is often construed as a signal that the current speaker is ready to give up his or her turn. So, if we wish to continue our speaking turn, we often need to fill the silences with a sound to show that we intend to carry on speaking.' But there probably aren't many linguistic experts in the corporate world, which is why when call centre staff are trained, they are instructed to avoid 'foghorning.' This is presumably because protracted 'eeeeer' sounds are a little like foghorns. Ok. But it's also perhaps unsurprising that speakers of different languages use different sounds as fillers, which renders the term meaningless when used in training notes for staff in call centres based in India. Imperialism – or unfathomable ignorance – remains rife.

It's on my Radar

A statement you'll hear countless times when travelling by train within earshot of a corporate cock is, "Yeah, yeah, it's on my radar..." A favourite of the inept and those who prefer to look busy rather than actually doing anything.

Car-Park That

I suspect that most normal people consider a car-park to be a large flat place where drivers park cars. The clue's in the name, really. But if someone says they're going to 'car-park that' during a meeting, it's probably not a good sign. On the surface, it's

Stay Cool... Chill... Get Down with the Kids

To me, a freezer is a domestic appliance that keeps foodstuffs cold, thus preserving them. The principle is extended in the business world to refer to keeping an idea fresh but inactive. Or something. A variation of the real-world term whereby something such as a project is put 'on ice,' putting it in the freezer is much snappier and inventive, and provides a neat alternative to car-parking, or a 'cooler' alternative to the back burner.

Skills, Hard and...?

Whatever your line of work, you need skills. Without skills, you can't do the job – whatever it may be. So, it stands to reason that companies need skilled employees, whatever their line of business, be it refuse collecting, shelf-stacking, pizza delivery, brain surgery or aeronautics. But it's only really in an office environment that you'll find people extolling the virtues of the staff wit the right 'soft skills.' According to a recent BBC report, 'many graduates lack soft skills.' But what are these skills, which, apparently, 'recognised as key to making businesses more profitable and better places to work' according to a number of sources? Perhaps unsurprisingly, the definition is as broad as to be near meaningless, as is often the case with the 'conceptual' aspect of business. Fundamentally, soft skills relate to a person's interpersonal skills, their possessing a responsible demeanour, their ability to self-manage, negotiate, and their levels of honesty and integrity. Of course, soft skills don't necessarily reflect one's ability to actually do the job. Moreover, if an interviewer simply isn't keen on an applicant, even if they have the best experience and are the best qualified for the job, they can turn them down with the excuse – sorry, justification – that they 'didn't possess the right soft skills.' And what the hell is a 'hard skill' is such a thing exists?

Be Progressive, B-E Progressive

The corporate world is big on buzzwords. Nevermind if they're meaningful or used sincerely. Image is everything. Substance is for other people to worry about. Yes, the box is empty, but it looks nice from the outside, so people are going to be happy to pay through the nose for it. And they're supposed to be thinking outside the box anyway, so what does it matter what's inside? Progressive is one such buzzword. Companies like to appear 'progressive' – whatever that means. As far as I can tell, it means they've found new ways of screwing people over and making as much profit as possible for delivering the minimum of service or product they can get away with.

Shift the Blame Through Blameshifting

You've fucked up. Royally. So royally you could probably even find yourself out of a job. Do you grovel for your life and your career? No, of course not. You point the finger. So-and-so fed me the wrong stats, or didn't provide them on schedule. So-and-so completely failed to touch base when he was supposed to, and consequently you had no idea he'd taken the project in completely the wrong tangent. So-and-so gets hauled over the coals, and your job is safe. Yes, let some other poor cunt take the heat. The blame.... has been shifted. And that... is blameshifting.

Pass the Buck

Sometimes there's no blame as such. But in business, you need the right tools, and the right support from the right people. Which, for those in higher management, means a lot of people who sit around and nod in agreement and make encouraging noises during meetings, agree to do everything suggested, and then delegate the task of actually doing what's been agreed to some poorly paid sucker further down the food chain. So, when progress is slower than the higher management wants, it's not the fault of the nodding, encouraging cronies. It's because the guys they delegated to aren't pulling their weight, or encountered various obstacles or 'blockages.' Ask the poorly paid sucker about the obstacles, and you'll find another, even more poorly paid sucker has encountered problems – IT issues, or all the staff on his department have been off sick or quit and not been replaced. On referring to IT or HR about their involvement, it will transpire there are budget issues. Probably a shortfall because someone in higher management is being a tightwad. And so it goes on, up and down, to and fro, along and along. Passing the buck can be a very effective career strategy, and doing it well without ever being caught without an excuse is a valuable skill. A soft one, no doubt.

Sporting Analogies

The use of sports analogies and terminology is as *de rigueur* in the business world as it is cringe-inducing. This is largely on account of phrases like 'stepping up to the plate' being used by middle-aged bozos who clearly have no interest in sport – or indeed anything outside of work – in order to build some kind of connection with their (usually younger) staff who do have outside interests. In the UK, it's bad enough when these so-not-down-with-the-kids-it-hurts management types make assumptions about the hobbies and interests of their staff and start shoehorning in references to 'goals' and 'getting over the line,' having 'a lot of hurdles,' 'jumping thruogh hoops' (for the sporting dolphins in the company) and 'getting a hole in one' and 'kabaddi kabaddi kabaddi' (ok, I made that one up), but when they use phrases that relate to sports not played – or watched – in the UK, the absurdity of the use of sports-related terms becomes particularly apparent.

Capture that Data!

The connotations of 'capture' to the majority of people, are, I would expect, suggestive of being caught or taking prisoners rather than suggesting anything to do with information. But given the way so much information gets misused and misinterpreted, it's perhaps fitting that to gather and record information and numbers is referred to as capturing the data. After all, you just know all that data's begging to be set free again....

Statistically Speaking...

Everyone knows that there are lies, damn lies, and statistics. But in business, statistics – or Stats – mean everything. Even when they mean nothing. They dress them up in pie-charts, graphs, Venn diagrams, wavy lines in different colours to show the targets and the actuality and waffle on at length about the way 'the figures speak for themselves' in board meetings and presentations, often without having even the vaguest grasp on what the crunched numbers are saying. And what are they saying? Well, precisely whatever whoever's presenting them wants to. It's all a matter of spin. Spin? No, glass half full / glass half empty! For example, when it's announced that the latest customer survey showed that 75% of respondents were happy with the service, it's often whooped up as a big positive. Cue huge round of back-slapping and ignore the fact that 25% of respondents to the same survey thought the service was gash. Until it's time for the annual reviews and the bonuses of the staff who actually do the work, at which point 25% of customers were dissatisfied, which is an unacceptable level, and is used to justify doling out paltry payouts and below-inflation annual increases.

Flow Charts and Process Maps

Planning is everything in business. Indeed, for some people, planning is a full-time job. But 'planning stuff' doesn't sound particularly sexy, and so to pretty things up, charts and illustrations – usually done on Powerpoint – are favoured by these tedious nerds. So, you want to know how something happens? Sure. But 'you go from A to C via B really isn't impressive, which is why jazzing things up with boxes connected by lines and arrows is the thing to do. But then, 'boxes connected by lines and arrows' doesn't sound too impressive either, which is why Flow Charts and Process Maps were invented. It makes the data you've captured look cool and sound cool and, better still, co-ordinated, rendering a haphazard pile of papers being shunted between desks a smooth, linear sequence of events. Clever huh?

...But is it Feasible?

Of course, not all questions have answers. And some questions cannot be answered with a simple, straightforward 'yes' or 'no.' But many can. In the real world, you may ask – or be asked – if 4 printers is enough between 800 people who are employed to write letters for 7 hours a day, 5 days a week. And the answer, based on simple logic and common sense would almost always be 'no' (followed by the exclamation 'of course not! What a ridiculous question!') but in the business world, it requires gathering a bunch of people together to discuss it, before setting out the objectives of a feasibility study. Usually, they'll spend a month coming up with a codename for the project, spend hours flouncing about and arranging 'telecons' and generally pricking about while failing to grasp the basic premise of what they're researching, only to conclude after six months that they need to gather more data to make a proper assessment. So next time you hear talk of feasibility, just say 'fuck it, I'll bring my own pencil sharpener from home.'

Acronymamania!

"Quick! I need a SOAP ASAP! And I need that MI PDQ, I'm in a telecon in five!" you've probably heard such things being said – or yelled – countless times by managers and management suck-ups if you happen to work in an office. If you know what the fuck they're on about, then it's a fair sign that you've probably been there for too long. Time is money. Using words takes time, and therefore costs money. Thus, to save money, acronyms can be immensely useful. Acronyms aren't terrible per se, and nor are they found exclusively in the business domain. But in the corporate environment, managers and people on projects have a habit of cooking up new ones and creating acronyms for things that probably don't really need or warrant acronyms behind closed doors and in exclusive meetings. "Yes, we need to really start pushing them on the Scheme for Outreach Directives, going forward... that way, we can really start Making a

Difference and provide Good Value for Money, going forward." Quite forgetting that these new terms aren't common knowledge, a mass communication will be circulated around the entire company, and it will be littered with these obscure sequences of capital letters without any explanation of their meaning: 'All staff, FYI: Project Beckham is pleased to announce that Bill McToss will be the CUNT going forward. PB's objectives are focused around our focus on SOD, which will enable us to facilitate a mode of operating whereby all staff will be able to MAD. We hope to see al staff MAD by the end of the year, and there will be MAD meetings held across all sites ITNF, because SOD is central to our FUCK and SHIT strategy in the next FY. Our new impetus is on GVFM and we hope to roll this out to all departments in the next 6 months going forward.'

Roll Up, Roll Up, Roll Out! Or, You Gotta Roll (Out) With It...

The word 'roll' has a number of meanings, according to the dictionary. It can be a cylinder, a small bread loaf, a list or register, or, when used as a verb, indicates turning over and over on an axis. However, in business speak, to 'roll out' means to introduce broadly. Of course, sometimes a 'roll-out' can be company wide, while others can see a small team of three our four adopt a new process, in which case said process is 'rolled out' to the team or department. The term has recently crossed into common parlance, and often appears in news stories. Indeed, a recent advertisement for an airliner stated that certain services – food, reclining seats, or somesuch – were being rolled out across all flights in the coming months. In light of this, the dominance of the term seems to suggest that rolling out may be analogous to the action of a steamroller.

High-Level Stuff

High Level – a phrase that clearly serves to reinforce the us and them division between managers and the chairpounders who aren't important enough or savvy enough to understand what the upper echelons of an organisation discuss behind closed doors. The meeting's all about high-level stuff... we'll break it down and roll it out to staff once we've fully digested the implications of the implementing the strategy moving forward. What they really mean is that because they don't actually do the work, they haven't got a clue, and so talk about things broadly and vaguely with no idea of whether or not it's physically possible. So, 'we need to make a saving in this area of £6.2M. If we reduce the staffing levels by 60% that should do it.' Yeah, but the work volume's still there. But that's not for the people on the shop floor whose jobs are on the line to worry about, because it's high level. The penpushing proles wouldn't understand.

Push the Envelope

The implications of pushing the envelope sound on the surface to be very like passing the buck. But no, It's going beyond the established boundaries. So why not pushing the boundaries or parameters rather than some meaningless metaphorical envelope?

Blag it Like Fuck

Sometimes there just isn't a carp metaphor or catchphrase that fits the bill. I've overheard managers on phone calls, in telecons or even in meetings foundering for a phrase that sounds impressive and serves to cover the fact they haven't a clue what they're talking about. "Yeah, yeah, I've not really got so far going forward on this one, it's got a lot of chefs on it and I didn't want to step on anyone's toes. I'm still trying to capture down the soft knowledge, and it's on my radar..." When you hear this, you just know something fishy's going down...

But why? Knowledge is power. If you know the code, are privy to the important, 'key concepts' you can speak in a manner that sets you apart from the plebs, the drones on the bottom rungs, and those who aren't in the world of business. And in doing so, it's possible to demonstrate that knowledge and radiate signals that you therefore have the power.

Memorise these and use them, as frequently as possible. Everyone will think you're a cock, but hey, you'll be on the board in no time.

'At Home He's a Tourist: Reconsidering the Postmodern Condition,' 'Get a Little Bit Closer: Memoir, Accessibility and Brushing Virtual Shoulders with Celebrity' and 'The Worker' first appeared in blog form on MySpace (http://www.myspace.com/christophernosnibor)

'Candidate' first appeared at badmarmalade.com

Parts of 'How to Get Ahead in Business' have appeared in various locations on line.

By the same author:

Bad Houses

THE PLAGIARIST

A Call for Submission

C.N.N. (With Stuart Bateman).

www.ingramcontent.com/pod-product-compliance
Lightning Source LLC
Chambersburg PA
CBHW031904170626

46807CB00004B/1892